HIP-HOP

Queen Latifah

Gail Snyder

Mason Crest Publishers

Queen Latifah

FRONTIS Rapper Queen Latifah, pictured here during a 2003 performance, has moved beyond her hip-hop roots to establish herself as a talented actress.

PRODUCED BY 21ST CENTURY PUBLISHING AND COMMUNICATIONS, INC.

MASON CREST PUBLISHERS INC.
370 Reed Road
Broomall, Pennsylvania 19008
(866)MCP-BOOK (toll free)
www.masoncrest.com

Printed in the U.S.A.

First Printing

9 8 7 6 5 4 3 2 1

Library of Congress Cataloging-in-Publication Data

Snyder, Gail.
   Queen Latifah / Gail Snyder.
      p. cm. — (Hip-hop)
   Includes bibliographical references and index.
   Hardback edition: ISBN-13: 978-1-4222-0126-8
   Hardback edition: ISBN-10: 1-4222-0126-0
   Paperback edition: ISBN-13: 978-1-4222-0276-0
   1. Latifah, Queen—Juvenile literature. 2. Rap musicians—United States—Biography—Juvenile literature. 3. Actresses—United States—Biography—Juvenile literature. I. Title. II. Series.
   ML3930.L178S68 2007
   782.421649092—dc22
   [B]   2006011446

Publisher's notes:
- All quotations in this book come from original sources, and contain the spelling and grammatical inconsistencies of the original text.

- The Web sites mentioned in this book were active at the time of publication. The publisher is not responsible for Web sites that have changed their addresses or discontinued operation since the date of publication. The publisher will review and update the Web site addresses each time the book is reprinted.

Contents

Hip-Hop Timeline

1974 Hip-hop pioneer Afrika Bambaataa organizes the Universal Zulu Nation.

1988 *Yo! MTV Raps* premieres on MTV.

1970s Hip-hop as a cultural movement begins in the Bronx, New York City.

1985 *Krush Groove*, a hip-hop film about Def Jam Recordings, is released featuring Run-D.M.C., Kurtis Blow, LL Cool J, and the Beastie Boys.

1970s DJ Kool Herc pioneers the use of breaks, isolations, and repeats using two turntables.

1979 The Sugarhill Gang's song "Rapper's Delight" is the first hip-hop single to go gold.

1986 Run-D.M.C. are the first rappers to appear on the cover of *Rolling Stone* magazine.

1970   1980   1988

1976 Grandmaster Flash & the Furious Five pioneer hip-hop MCing and freestyle battles.

1986 Beastie Boys' album *Licensed to Ill* is released and becomes the best-selling rap album of the 1980s.

1970s Break dancing emerges at parties and in public places in New York City.

1982 Afrika Bambaataa embarks on the first European hip-hop tour.

1988 Hip-hop music annual record sales reaches $100 million.

1970s Graffiti artist Vic pioneers tagging on subway trains in New York City.

1984 *Graffiti Rock*, the first hip-hop television program, premieres.

1993 Rapper Snoop Dogg's album *Doggystyle* is the first debut album to hit the music charts at number one.

2006 Queen Latifah becomes the first hip-hop artist to receive a star on the Hollywood Walk of Fame.

1989 DJ Jazzy Jeff & The Fresh Prince become the first hip-hop artists to win a Grammy Award.

2003 Rapper Eminem becomes the first hip-hop artist to win an Academy Award.

2005 Hip-hop artist Kanye West appears on the cover of *Time* magazine.

1989 Rap is added as a new category to the *Billboard* charts.

1997 East Coast rapper Notorious B.I.G. (aka Biggie Smalls) is murdered.

2004 First National Hip-Hop Political Convention is held in Newark, New Jersey.

1989

2000

2006

1990s Hip-hop emerges in Europe.

1996 West Coast rapper Tupac Shakur is shot and killed.

2005 Rapper Will Smith opens the Philadelphia Live 8 concert as part of 10 simultaneous concerts held worldwide to bring attention to the extreme poverty in Africa.

1989 First gangsta rap album, *Straight Outta Compton*, is released by N.W.A.

2001 The hip-hop political action group, Hip-Hop Summit Action Network, is founded by Russell Simmons.

2006 The Smithsonian Institute National Museum of American History announces the creation of a new hip-hop exhibition scheduled to open in three to five years.

1992 Dr. Dre's album *The Chronic* is released; it redefines West Coast rap.

On January 4, 2006, singer and actor Queen Latifah became the first hip-hop artist recognized with a star on the Hollywood Walk of Fame. Here, she celebrates the unveiling of her star on the famous walkway.

Honored with a Star

On January 4, 2006, hip-hop icon Queen Latifah knelt on the sidewalk near Grauman's Chinese Theatre in Hollywood, California, with a wide smile on her face. Although she did not realize it, she was doing something no other hip-hop artist had ever done: posing with the bronze star signifying her entry into the Hollywood Walk of Fame.

It was Queen Latifah Day in Hollywood, a moment that came nearly 20 years after the rapper first appeared on the hip-hop scene as one of the first female MCs. After proving that she could succeed in the music world, Latifah stepped in front of the camera. She starred in a hit television series, hosted her own talk show, became a model in high-profile commercials for Cover Girl and Wal-Mart, and appeared in more than 30 movies, sometimes alongside some of the most famous actors in Hollywood.

Queen Latifah became the 2,298th person to receive a star on the 46-year-old walk, which honors greats from radio, television, movies, music, and theater. The 18-block walk is located on one of the most famous streets in America, Hollywood Boulevard. It was started in 1958 as a project to improve the face of Hollywood and has since been named a cultural landmark by the City of Los Angeles.

The Walk of Fame is a major tourist attraction and gathering place for fans, who regard each star as an extension of the celebrity it represents. Visitors who happen upon the walk on John Lennon's birthday, for instance, will find a group of his fans assembled to honor the slain Beatle's memory. People make pilgrimages to visit the stars of performers who impacted their lives.

Recognized as a Movie Performer

Queen Latifah was the first celebrity to receive a star in 2006. Also honored that year were comedian Steve Martin, Latifah's costar in one of her most successful box office films, *Bringing Down the House*; actors Matthew Broderick, Holly Hunter, and Nathan Lane; recording artist Isaac Hayes; and the rock group Motley Crüe. Each star on the Hollywood Walk of Fame is adorned with one of five symbols depicting the field in which the person has been recognized. Queen Latifah's star bears the emblem of the movie camera, honoring her contributions to the film industry.

With her mother, friends, and actor Terrence Howard at her side, the 35-year-old performer received a plaque with a smaller version of the star from Leron Gubler, president of the Hollywood Chamber of Commerce. The Grammy-winning, Oscar-nominated MC was surprised to discover that she was the first hip-hop star to be given a place in the Walk of Fame. She thought the rapper-actor Will Smith had broken that barrier years before.

The Walk of Fame honor was a sign that Queen Latifah and hip-hop itself had become an integral part of **mainstream** America. The music performers who had once only attracted the attention of inner city youths were now routinely showing up in movies, television commercials, newspapers, and magazine stories.

Rap Becomes Mainstream

Filmmaker Larron Tate explained the trend to a reporter for the newspaper *Red Eye*:

"Studios see that adding a rapper to the cast can bring in a lot of revenue. They think they're basically guaranteed to add an urban audience to the picture.... People in other countries see these rappers on tour, buy their music, so they know them. They will put up money to see them in theaters, whereas they may not do that for an unfamiliar African-American actor."

Queen Latifah, surrounded by members of her family, holds a plaque representing her Walk of Fame star. From left are Latifah's sister, Raven Owens; her mother, Rita Owens; Queen Latifah; her father, Lance Owens; and her brother, Angelo Owens.

Since John Singleton's *Boyz N the Hood*, starring Ice Cube, studios have embraced hiring rappers. Rappers LL Cool J, Snoop Dogg, Eminem, Ludacris, and DMX have all found work in the movies. But none of them have worked alongside the kind of traditional Hollywood talent that Queen Latifah has. She has appeared with such box office draws as Dustin Hoffman, Steve Martin, Denzel Washington, Catherine Zeta-Jones, and Renee Zellweger.

Receiving a star on the Hollywood Walk of Fame was an emotional moment for Queen Latifah. "It was something you always dream about," she told reporters. Though she initially gained fame as a singer, Queen Latifah's star honored her acting work.

The first time Queen Latifah visited the Hollywood Walk of Fame she was 17 years old. She had flown across the country with her mother from her New Jersey home to visit her grandmother and a friend she knew from school. "It was kind of cool to see all these names here, so to be part of that is crazy." Queen Latifah told a reporter:

> **❝It was something you always dream about that you like [and] you want but you never know these things will happen. I was excited, because it's something that you share with everyone. It's not like winning a Golden Globe or an Oscar or SAG [Screen Actors Guild] award where you keep it and you have it in your mother's house or your house. This is something where everybody can walk up and down the street and go 'Oh, Queen Latifah.'❞**

Look Out World, Here She Comes

Queen Latifah also seized the moment to shine a spotlight on other female rappers, who even today have a hard time breaking into the male-dominated industry. "I think the reason I am here is to inspire African-American women who are rappers, full-figured women to know they can do it, too," she told a reporter for the Associated Press. At Queen Latifah's side was her mother, Rita Owens. Owens always inspired her daughter to be whoever she wanted to be. Owens told reporters: "Who would have known that in the '70s, when a pink 8-pound baby girl was born, this is where she would be today. She came out screaming, 'Look out world, here I come.'"

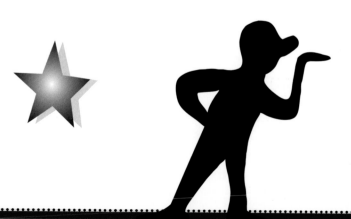

Queen Latifah pauses for a photo with her father at the 2004 MTV Movie Awards. Lance Owens was a Vietnam War veteran and police officer in Newark, New Jersey, when his daughter, Dana, was born in 1970.

2

Tomboy to Tommy Boy

Dana Elaine Owens was born on March 18, 1970, in Newark, New Jersey, a city just across the river from New York City. There were three main influences in her young life: her father, her mother, and the emerging hip-hop culture and music that provided the daily soundtrack to her life.

Her father, Lancelot Owens, was a Newark policeman who admired Black Panthers like Huey Newton, Stokely Carmichael, and Bobby Seale. The Black Panthers were a 1960s-era radical group that believed in using violent resistance to achieve equality with whites. Because of this, their leaders often ran afoul of the law. Nevertheless, the group's overall message—that blacks could empower themselves to achieve equality—was admired and adopted by many in the community. The message of black power was familiar to Dana because her father would often discuss racial relations when his friends visited. To young Dana, her father was a hero. He was a Vietnam veteran who practiced martial arts. He taught her to appreciate camping and the outdoors, and told her that she could do anything a boy could do. He was "cool, respected, handsome, gentle to me as his daughter," she said.

Dana's mother, Rita Owens, had grown up an artistic child in a family too big to nourish her talent. She vowed to do everything she could to help her own children achieve their potential. When her son Lance wanted to take karate, her daughter asked if she could go as well. Rita agreed. Dana was a tomboy and always ready for a game of baseball or basketball with the boys.

Living in the Projects

Queen Latifah's mother recalled, "I learned early on just what Dana wasn't. When she was little, I would dress her in prissy outfits, complete with bows in her hair and matching bobby socks. By the end of the day, the bows would be either missing or knocked to the side and the socks rolled down and dirty. She'd have chocolate around her mouth and spots on her dress. I knew then there was no use forcing my daughter to be dainty. She was who she was. I got a dynamo."

The Owens household was a musical one. Lancelot Owens would play the bongos and conga drums in **jam sessions** with his friends. No one minded when Dana and her brother beat on pots and pans right along with the adults. Dana was also exposed to reggae, jazz, salsa, rhythm and blues, and artists like Patti LaBelle, Sarah Vaughn, and Dinah Washington.

But the Owens household also had its problems. While Rita and Lancelot Owens loved each other, their marriage had difficulties. Queen Latifah told reporters that she never recalled her parents fighting, "If our parents ever argued, it wasn't around us." But when Rita could no longer tolerate her husband's infidelities and drug use, the couple separated and eventually divorced. Dana was eight when the separation became final. She recalls:

❝**One day my parents sat us down, and Mom said 'We're going to separate. Daddy's going to live somewhere else.' We were crushed. What did we do wrong? Did we not clean our room enough? It affected me more because of how much it hurt my brother. He didn't want any man to replace our father. In many ways, I was more independent than Winki— maybe tougher than he was, less introverted and introspective.**❞

Rita Owens, Dana's mother, struggled to raise her children in a tough inner-city neighborhood. Rita was an artistic woman, and she wanted all of her children to fulfill their potential. She often encouraged Dana to express herself through music, as well as to study hard.

LADIES FIRST
REVELATIONS OF A STRONG WOMAN
QUEEN LATIFAH

Queen Latifah discussed her childhood experiences in her 2000 biography *Ladies First*. Reviewers praised the book. "Latifah's positive 'be yourself' attitude is infectious," wrote *Publishers Weekly*. "Readers are bound to come away from this book wanting—at least a little bit—to be like Latifah."

There were hard times for Rita and her two children after the break-up. The family was forced to move into public housing. Rita worked several part-time jobs until she had enough money to move to a more prosperous neighborhood. She also started attending Essex County College, so she could become a high school art teacher.

Recalling her childhood, Queen Latifah told James Lipton of *Inside the Actors Studio*, "For the most part it was OK. But I think that anybody who grows up in a housing project in any-town USA is going to be exposed to a lot of things they probably shouldn't be exposed to: violence, drugs, cliques. You know what I mean. I could join them or stay separated from them or fight—you know, have to stand up for yourself."

Becoming Latifah

When Dana was eight, her cousin Sharonda paid a fateful visit. Both girls wanted to choose Muslim names like their friends were doing. This had become a popular way for young African Americans to identify and express a sense of self. Sharonda brought over a book of Muslim names with accompanying definitions. Dana settled on Latifah, which means "delicate, sensitive, and kind." While she may have been a tomboy, she felt that the name described her true self. Fighting with boys and excelling at sports was what she did, not who she was. According to her mother, "Dana's daintiness was internal. She had softness and gentleness. . . . If you told Dana she had disappointed you, she would shed tears." Sharonda's younger sister was also named Latifah, and Dana thought it was beautiful. In her autobiography, *Ladies First*, she wrote:

> **"For me, Latifah was freedom. I loved the name my parents gave me, Dana Elaine Owens. But I knew then that something as simple as picking a new name for myself would be my first act of defining who I was— for myself and for the world. *Dana* was daughter. *Dana* was sister. *Dana* was student, friend, girl in the 'hood. But *Latifah* was someone else. She would belong only to me. It was more than a persona. Becoming Latifah would give me the autonomy to be what I *chose* to be—without being influenced by anyone else's expectations of what a young girl from Newark is supposed to be. Or what she is supposed to do. Or what she is supposed to want."**

Dana was a gifted student who attended mainly Catholic schools where she was active in school plays and athletics. She received a standing **ovation** for her performance as Dorothy in *The Wiz*, an updated, hip version of *The Wizard of Oz*. In her sophomore year, she transferred to Irvington Public High School. At 5 feet 9 inches tall, she was a key member of the girls' basketball team, which won two state championships. She was popular in high school, voted the Best All-Around, Best Dancer, and Most Popular student.

Dana's mother, who had gone back to college to obtain a teaching degree, taught art at Irvington. While some teens might have been embarrassed to attend a school in which their parent was a teacher, Dana was thrilled. Her mom was considered the "cool teacher," and through her influence the already popular teenager became friends with classmates who would help launch her career in hip-hop. Some of them are still working with the superstar today.

In geometry class Dana met Joseph Compere, now known as "Shakim," who became her long-time business partner. Because Rita Owens booked DJs for school parties, she was able to introduce Dana to a DJ named "Mark the 45 King." The two clicked. Dana began hanging out in Mark's basement with his friends. She was the youngest in the posse and the only girl, so she began referring to herself as the "Princess of the Posse."

"I was really curious about life and what I could do," Queen Latifah told a reporter for *Parade* magazine. "I'd listen to beats and write rhymes and sing them for the guys. We'd talk and dream for hours about being rappers and starting businesses."

Flipping Burgers for Hip-Hop Money

Latifah got a job at a local Burger King so she could have money to buy rap records and attend rap performances. She was excited about earning money for herself and still recalls the amount of her first paycheck: $88. One of her favorite places to see performances was the Latin Quarters, on the corner of 48th Street and Broadway in New York City. The now-closed hip-hop club helped launch the careers of Run-D.M.C. and Salt-N-Pepa. To get inside, Latifah would often have to stand in a long line that stretched for blocks. Sometimes she would even sneak out of the house to get there.

Meanwhile, in Mark's basement, Latifah and her friends continued their school of rap, critiquing each other's performances. One of her

Dana Owens was a talented basketball player in high school, and helped her team win two state championships. Here, she stars in a humorous sketch about basketball with famed player Cheryl Miller on the television show *In Living Color*.

best friends, a Liberian immigrant named Ramsey, was especially influential. He was older than Latifah, who was only 17, and already had a place of his own and a small amount of savings. Ramsey believed that Latifah was ready to make a demo tape and gave her $700 to cut a record entitled "Princess of the Posse."

In the world of hip-hop, demos cut by young, unknown talent often circulate among radio station DJs, who are constantly in search of cutting-edge performers to introduce to their audiences. Unknown to Latifah, her "Princess of the Posse" demo had been passed around, finally finding airtime on New York City radio station. In the summer of 1987, Latifah was listening to the radio in the family's apartment above the Modern Era Barber Shop in East Orange, New Jersey, a city in the northern part of the state about 20 miles from New York, when she heard "Princess of the Posse."

One of Dana's favorite hip-hop groups was Run-D.M.C., which included Darryl "D.M.C." McDaniel, Joseph "DJ Run" Simmons, and Jason "Jam Master Jay" Mizell. During the early 1980s, the group became one of the first hip-hop acts to receive mainstream attention and radio airplay.

Her record was being played by one of her favorite DJs, and the news was too good to keep to herself.

"Our apartment had windows on both Halsted and Elmwood Avenues. I ran from one side to the other screaming down the streets, 'My record is on the radio! My record is on the radio!' I'm sure I woke up half the neighborhood. But I didn't care. My record was on the radio. I hadn't even officially signed with a label. And they were playing my song on the radio. My dream had been realized."

Of course her dream was only beginning. Mark the 45 King gave Latifah's demo to Fab Five Freddy, the host of *Yo! MTV Raps*. Fab Five Freddy passed it on to Dante Ross at Tommy Boy Records. The staff at Tommy Boy liked what they heard as well. Much to her surprise, Latifah found herself on the phone with the president of the record label. He had one question: Would she like a record contract?

IS THE "N" WORD COOL WITH YOU?

THE SOURCE

THE MAGAZINE OF HIP-HOP MUSIC, CULTURE & POLITICS

QUEEN LATIFAH

BORN 2 ROLL

HONDA

HEAVY D • WARREN G
SHYHEIM THE RUGGED CHILD
THE LOST ART OF FREESTYLING

MAY 1994 NO. 56
US $2.95 • UK £1.95 • CANADA $3.50
05

Queen Latifah is featured on the cover of the May 1994 issue of *The Source* magazine, a publication devoted to hip-hop music and culture. By this time, she had already released several successful and critically acclaimed albums.

3

The Queen Has Arrived

Just a teenager when she broke into the national hip-hop scene, Dana Owens was no overnight success. She took music and dance lessons and worked on her rapping style as a member of the high school hip-hop group Ladies Fresh. She read rap magazines cover to cover and soaked up the New York rap scene.

However, all of the available role models were male. Latifah was the only girl rapping in Mark's basement, and she rarely saw women perform in the clubs. Seeing Salt-N-Pepa, an all-female group, perform at the Latin Quarters was encouraging. But still, Salt-N-Pepa's glamorous ladies were not easy for Latifah to identify with.

All that changed when the Quarters hosted Sweet T and Jazzy Joyce. These were two women Latifah could really relate to. Sweet T and Jazzy Joyce performed in the same sweat suits she favored. There was no pretense at all—just solid music and the crowd loved it.

While Sweet T and Jazzy Joyce proved that someone like Latifah could make it in hip-hop, the young rapper was not counting on making hip-hop a career. In fact, she had settled on becoming a lawyer or journalist and was enrolled at a junior college when she landed her record contract. The contract changed everything. She'd been given a rare opportunity to follow a dream and decided to quit school and put her soul into performing.

When Tommy Boy signed her in 1988, she had the chance to reconsider what she wanted to call herself. Dana had already become Latifah, but a recording name needed more. At the time, a lot of rappers were calling themselves MCs, but Latifah wanted to set herself apart in as many ways as she could.

A Positive Message

Dana settled on "Queen Latifah" not only because she liked how it sounded but also because her mother had impressed upon her that all women are deserving of the respect given to royalty. This was a message Queen Latifah thought African-American women needed to hear. "A queen is a queen when riding high, and when clouded in disgrace, shame, or sorrow, she has dignity. Being a queen has very little to do with exterior things. It is a state of mind," she wrote in *Ladies First*.

She made other important decisions, too. She decided she would write **lyrics** that lifted women up without putting men down. She would avoid using profanities and references to drugs and create an on-stage look for herself that did not rely on sex appeal to sell her songs.

She told *New York* magazine, "Sex sells; that's common sense. A lot of women sell their bodies—without *selling* them. It shows you're lacking in talent. Positivity takes a bigger push. A lot of groups will curse just because they think it will sell. My *positivity* can sell."

Queen Latifah joined a collective effort called the Native Tongues featuring Monie Love, De La Soul, the Jungle Brothers, Kool D.J. Red Alert, and A Tribe Called Quest. The collective's message was "peace and love—'tribe vibes.'" They believed hip-hop could celebrate more than the worst of street culture and violence. Native Tongues were heavily influenced by rap pioneer Afrika Bambaataa, one of the best-known DJs in hip-hop and the first **impresario** to take hip-hop acts to Europe.

Tommy Boy used "Princess of the Posse" on the first Queen Latifah single the company produced. The flip side of the record was the song, "Wrath of My Madness." The next single released by Tommy Boy was Queen Latifah's "Dance for Me," which also included "Inside Out" on the flip side. These early records sold about 40,000 copies—enough for

Salt-N-Pepa was one of the first successful female hip-hop acts, recording several hits in the late 1980s and early 1990s. Although Queen Latifah was a fan, her own performing persona was quite different from Salt-N-Pepa's sexy, glamorous style.

Latifah's reputation to take hold. These songs contained boasts about her rapping style as "the Queen of royal badness" and the superior beats of DJ Mark.

She began making videos to support her records. For the song "Ladies First," Queen Latifah invited other female rappers to share the spotlight with her, a rap first. She had a generous attitude and did not consider other rappers to be competition. These early videos also showed a flair for the dramatic. In one featuring images of South African women, she is seen replacing white men on a chessboard with black power symbols.

Grammy Nomination

In 1989 Tommy Boy released Queen Latifah's first album, *All Hail the Queen*, which featured her early singles. It was nominated for a Grammy Award—a rare achievement for a first-time recording artist. In addition the New Music Seminar in Manhattan, an annual gathering of musicians and managers, named her Best New Artist of 1990.

The music press endorsed the album. *CMJ New Music Report* wrote, "Male rappers step off, because the Queen has arrived." A reviewer for *The New York Times*, which listed the album as a notable new release, commented, "The backup tracks are sometimes rich enough to carry the album, but they don't have to. Queen Latifah provides high-speed, syncopated rapping virtuosity."

All Hail the Queen eventually sold a million copies, and Queen Latifah gained an audience for her songs about women's rights, poverty, and segregation in South Africa. The standout single on the album, "Ladies First," was Queen Latifah's first **anthem** for women. It contains these lyrics:

> **"Who said that the ladies couldn't make it?**
> **You must be blind**
> **If you don't believe well here listen to this rhyme**
> **Ladies First there's no time to rehearse**
> **I'm divine and my mind expands through the universe**
> **A female rapper with a message to send."**

When Queen Latifah performed that song before live audiences, women cheered. While happy with the press she was receiving and the attention from fans, Queen Latifah was less thrilled that her pro-woman

The influential DJ Afrika Bambaataa is considered one of the founders of the hip-hop movement, and recorded the groundbreaking hit "Planet Rock." Bambaataa believed that hip-hop could be a positive force for social change—a vision Queen Latifah also shared.

message led to her being called a **feminist** by members of the media. She told a reporter for *New York*:

> **"** I just want to be me . . . I have a fear of feminism. To me feminists were usually white women who hated men. A lot seemed to be gay. They were always fightin'. I don't want to be that. The media showed

them that way [and the image has] never gone away. I don't want to be classified with them. What I have is common sense. I don't want chivalry to be dead. I want to have a man who will pull the chair out for me. I wanna grow old with somebody."

Queen Latifah delivers a lyric during a performance. Her straightforward delivery and carefully crafted rhymes drew critical praise after the release of her first album, *All Hail the Queen*, in 1989. That year, the record reached number six on *Billboard* magazine's Top Hip-Hop Albums chart.

However, after appearing on a panel with feminist speakers at Harvard University, Latifah decided that the label could apply to her. Those women expressed opinions she agreed with, opinions found in her lyrics. Latifah's lyrics gave young women an image of themselves as something other than the "ho" so often described in male rapper's lyrics.

Queen Latifah was different from other hip-hop artists in another way, too. Not only did she rap on her debut album, she sang and mixed in beats that could be classified as reggae, rhythm and blues, and dance party. The music itself was a different style.

In 1992 Tommy Boy released Queen Latifah's second album, *Nature of a Sista*. Once again Queen Latifah received a Grammy nomination for Best Solo Rap Performance. This time it was for the song "Fly Girl."

Queen Latifah told *The Village Voice* newspaper, "For *Nature of a Sista* I really wanted to just do the album and not think about what people expected of me, what people wanted for their damn selves, because people try to involve business into it and that stunts my creativity."

During production of the album, Queen Latifah and Tommy Boy executives had some artistic differences. When record sales did not meet Tommy Boy's expectations, the company did not renew her contract. This was the first real setback of her career.

Although Queen Latifah's career was taking off in the early 1990s, she was devastated by the death of her brother Lance in a 1992 motorcycle accident. She tried to ease the pain through alcohol and drugs, but eventually stopped her self-destructive behavior.

4

Guilt, Shame, Pain, and Fame

Touring and recording is exhausting work. Being away from home leaves artists drained and stressed, and Queen Latifah is no exception. For her, spending time with family and friends is an essential way to relax and unwind; so is finding the time to get behind the handlebars of her Honda motorcycle and cruise the open road.

Her passion for motorcycles was something she shared with her brother Lance. In 1992 she bought him a bike similar to hers for his birthday. She could afford to be generous. Her music and movie careers were taking off, and she had just signed a contract to record for Motown Records.

A day after Lance received the motorcycle from his sister, the unthinkable happened. He was hit by a car and a short time later died from his injuries. He was 24. Queen Latifah was heartbroken and depressed. Overnight, her life went into a tailspin. She told *Parade* magazine:

> **"His death was terrible. . . . When I lost him like that—suddenly, unexpectedly, in the prime of his life—the foundation of my life was just swept away. After that, you don't trust anything. . . . I was medicating every day, numbing the pain. I couldn't turn it off. I was getting high, I was getting drunk. Every day. It took five years before I could really feel anything else again."**

Brushes with the Law

As she worked out her pain, Queen Latifah found strength in her music. Her album *Black Reign*, the first she released after the tragedy, contained the song "Winki's Theme" as well as other cuts that expressed her loss. The single "U.N.I.T.Y." from *Black Reign* topped the charts. It won a Grammy for Best Solo Rap performance, an NAACP Image Award, and a *Soul Train* Music Award. Queen Latifah did not boast about these accomplishments. She said:

> **"I wrote it because all around I saw women being verbally and physically assaulted, especially in rap music. Gangsta rap was ruling at the time, and with it came all this . . . bull—*bitch* this, *ho* that. And crazy as it sounds, I saw female rappers buying into it. There was even a group that called itself BWA—Bitches with Attitude. . . . [T]hese ladies didn't even defend themselves in their music. . . . What kind of a message was that sending?"**

There were more dark days ahead. In 1995 Latifah and her friends Sean Moon and Lynn Mayo were carjacked at gunpoint at 2:45 AM in Harlem. Despite the fact that the passengers complied with their demands, the carjackers opened fire. Moon was shot in the stomach and had to undergo emergency surgery.

Queen Latifah also had a few brushes with the law herself. In 1996 she was arrested for speeding, marijuana possession, and carrying an unregistered gun. She took responsibility for her actions and was placed on three years' **probation**. Another charge of reckless driving was leveled against her in 2002, this time in Hollywood, for making an unsafe lane change. She received three years' probation for that offense as well.

Queen Latifah
Black Reign

This is the cover of Queen Latifah's third album, *Black Reign*, which was released in 1993. The album's biggest hit was the single "U.N.I.T.Y.," which reached number two on *Billboard*'s Hot Rap Singles chart in 1994.

In 1998 Motown released her album *Order in the Court*. In an interview with *Jet* magazine, Queen Latifah described the album:

> **"[I]t's almost like me calling order to hip hop. It needs some kind of balance. It needs the positive along with the rest of the stuff. It needs a different point of view, a**

different point of creativity that makes my stuff a little different from everybody else's."

Order in the Court turned out to be Queen Latifah's last rap album. Her next album, recorded some six years later, was the self-titled *Dana Owens Album* in which she recorded jazz, soul, and pop standards. "I've never wanted to be put into a box, not musically," she told National Public Radio.

While hip-hop made Queen Latifah an international star, her ambitious nature sought out other creative avenues. She wanted to show the world that Dana Owens had more talent than they knew. As she explained to National Public Radio:

Erika Alexander, Queen Latifah, Kim Field, and Kim Coles get down in a scene from the television show *Living Single*. Queen Latifah starred on the popular sitcom from 1993 until the show was canceled in 1997.

"In a funny way, I think I've always been trying to show people who I really am. There's a whole lot left for you to know about me. But I've been trying to spoon-feed people who I am, because I don't think I could give it to everybody all at once."

Living Single

Her big break outside the hip-hop world came when she won the role of Khadijah James in *Living Single*, a Fox television sitcom that ran from 1993 to 1997. On the popular network primetime show, Queen Latifah played a professional black woman who bore more resemblance to Dana Owens than her rap star **persona**. In a role written for her, Queen Latifah was cast as the owner of a magazine called *Flavor*, a nod to her real-life entertainment management company, Flavor Unit.

In 1999 Queen Latifah received another opportunity—the chance to host her own talk show. She was a brash newcomer competing against Oprah Winfrey and other more experienced hosts. *The Queen Latifah Show*, which earned respectable ratings, continued to express her love for rap as hip-hop stars DMX, Snoop Dogg, and Foxy Brown turned up on her guest list. At the height of its popularity, it drew some 2 million viewers per day.

With one successful project after another, Queen Latifah was laying the foundation for a significant movie career: one that would take her from bit player to star to behind-the-scenes creative roles, such as being a movie **producer.**

Queen Latifah poses in front of a large replica of the Oscar statuette at the Academy Awards Nominees' Luncheon, March 2003. She was nominated for a Best Supporting Actress Oscar for her performance as Mama Morton in the 2002 musical *Chicago*.

Academy Award Nominee

Queen Latifah has appeared in more than 30 films, earning her enough clout in the movie industry to pick and choose her roles. She has played sassy sisters, cab drivers, prison matrons, and jazz singers. Some of her movies have been comedies, some dramas, and some musicals. And now she produces movies in addition to starring in them.

Many of Queen Latifah's movie roles involved other stars from the rap world. In *Set It Off* she worked with Dr. Dre, while in *Barbershop 2* and *Beauty Shop* she worked with Ice Cube. In the movie *Brown Sugar*, her co-star was Mos Def, and in *Last Holiday*, she played the girlfriend of LL Cool J's character. Queen Latifah believes most rappers are natural actors. "We have to kind of make our case in two-and-a-half minutes or four minutes in a video," she told James Lipton of *Inside The Actors Studio*. She also said the fierce competition normally apparent between rappers is an asset when it comes to acting because they naturally strive to do their best.

A Serious Actress

In an interview with the BBC, Queen Latifah said, "In the early films I was just Queen Latifah. I had to start looking for parts that went against the grain because the movies I was offered were offshoots of Queen Latifah—strong sister, cursin'. I got an acting coach and decided to take it seriously because I wanted to get better. But I will never forget those directors who took a chance on me before I was trained because they saw some natural talent."

Queen Latifah has embraced acting as a challenge. She set her sights high and has been rewarded. "This film business is a challenge to me," she once said. "I want to be De Niro. I want to be Pacino and Foster and Hanks—but black. And I've got to put in work to do that."

Queen Latifah's earliest roles in such movies as *House Party 2, Juice,* and *Jungle Fever* were small. It was not until 1996 and the movie *Set It Off* that her career really blossomed. She played a **lesbian** named Cleo, who with three other friends turned to robbing banks to supplement the income they made cleaning houses. Queen Latifah also recorded songs for the movie's soundtrack. The film, which also starred Jada Pinkett Smith, Vivica Fox, and Kimberly Elise, was praised for its honest depiction of real black women struggling against poverty. In her book *Check It While I Wreck It: Black Womanhood, Hip-Hop Culture, and the Public Sphere,* college professor Gwendolyn D. Pough wrote, "The characters in this film all represent complicated variations and mixtures of the ghetto girl trio. And the film, although it was directed by a man, does not decenter the stories of these women or offer caricatured representations of Black womanhood."

In 1997 Queen Latifah played opposite Dustin Hoffman, Sharon Stone, and Samuel L. Jackson in *Sphere,* a science fiction movie. Of her role as a Navy diver in the film, Queen Latifah told the *New York Times*: "It's not a big role, but it's a great cast. I like to work around people who can stretch me. I need competition to grow. It's like playing basketball. You can't get better if you don't play with the best."

The following year she honed her talents further by working with Danny DeVito and Holly Hunter in the comedy *Living Out Loud.* Queen Latifah played nightclub singer Liz Bailey, a friend to Hunter's character. The role once again allowed Queen Latifah to utilize her vocal talents. Critic Sharon Johnson, writing in the Harrisburg *Patriot News*, said, "Queen Latifah takes a giant step forward as an actress and musician in the role of a lounge singer with great taste in songs, deplorable taste in men. Listening to the rapper's take on some jazz and rhythm and blues classics is pure pleasure."

In 1999 Queen Latifah appeared in the thriller *The Bone Collector* with Denzel Washington, Angelina Jolie, and Michael Rooker. Her supporting role as a nurse for Washington's character, a paralyzed police detective trying to find a serial killer, was praised by movie critic Roger Ebert for its "good energy."

Queen Latifah's most stunning contribution to movies so far has been her portrayal of prison matron Mama Morton in the movie *Chicago* (2002), which required her to sing, act, and dance with stars Richard Gere, Renee Zellweger, and Catherine Zeta-Jones. The performance led to her becoming the first rap singer nominated for an

Cedric the Entertainer gets an earful from Queen Latifah as Ice Cube watches in a scene from *Barbershop 2* (2004). A sequel to a surprise hit from 2002, *Barbershop 2* was modestly successful, earning more than $65 million.

Academy Award for Best Supporting Actress. She was also nominated for a Golden Globe and took home an NAACP Image Award for the role. Such recognition would be a high point in any career, and Queen Latifah was as thrilled as she had been as a teenager when she first heard her song on the radio. "I feel really good and proud and surprised and excited," she told a reporter from *Jet*.

> **"I jumped around and hollered and screamed. I tried to call my mother. Tried to call my dad. You always hope for these things. But there are so many talented people out there, and so many good movies, I am just glad to have my name thrown in the mix."**

Queen Latifah performs her Oscar-nominated song from *Chicago* **with costar Catherine Zeta-Jones at the Academy Awards ceremony in March 2003. Although Queen Latifah did not win the Oscar for Best Supporting Actress, she was thrilled and honored to be nominated.**

Queen Latifah had to fight for the role of Mama Morton, auditioning three times. She beat out Bette Midler, Rosie O'Donnell, and Kathy Bates. Mama reminded Queen Latifah of her own grandmother, who died while the movie was being filmed. "I feel like my grandmother was that Mama Morton character, you know?" she said in an interview with *CBS News.* "She was a big-breasted, sexy woman that was a pistol!" *Entertainment Weekly* summed up her performance in the film:

❝With her wryly hard-boiled demeanor and regal-yet-streetwise carriage—and that ever-present sly twinkle in her eyes—Latifah brings a refreshing new dimension to this lovably unlovable character. Large and in charge, Latifah proves she's the boss with the hot sauce. And this gal can sing, too, as her show-stopping rendition of 'When You're Good to Mama' eloquently attests.❞

Taking Some Heat

In *Brown Sugar*, released in 2002, Queen Latifah played Francine, the best friend of a woman who edits a hip-hop magazine. Once again, Queen Latifah was called upon to be the funny friend of the movie's main character. But with *Bringing Down the House*, released in 2003, she emerged as a leading lady. The film, which also starred Steve Martin and Eugene Levy, grossed $130 million. However, it troubled some critics who found her role as sassy jail breaker Charlene Morton to be filled with **stereotypes**. Among those who criticized her performance was Renee Graham of the *Boston Globe*, who wrote:

❝As Charlene, she spews more slang than a week's worth of episodes of BET's *106 & Park*. She solves her problems with violence (a prolonged bathroom beat-down of Martin's former sister-in-law is appalling) and spends most of her time being as loud and ignorant as possible. Worst of all, her character is little more than the latest, lamest spin on Hollywood's Magic Negro, with Latifah solving all kinds of problems for the boring white suburban folks. She teaches Martin's son to read, exacts revenge against his daughter's overly aggressive boyfriend, and kick-starts Martin's

love life—but, of course, not with her. She's presented as an exotic creature, a hip-hop Hottentot Venus to be ogled and objectified.**"**

In 2005 Queen Latifah co-produced *Beauty Shop* in which she continued her role as Gina Norris from the earlier *Barbershop 2* movie. This time Queen Latifah's character received major screen time as a widow trying to make a good life for her 11-year-old daughter in Atlanta by starting her own beauty shop. Queen Latifah shared this movie with a big cast including Kevin Bacon, Alicia Silverstone, Alfre Woodard, and Andie MacDowell. Ty Burr of the *Boston Globe* wrote:

Steve Martin and Eugene Levy perform with Queen Latifah in a scene from 2003's *Bringing Down the House*. The comedy made a lot of money, but some people criticized the film for its stereotypical characters.

Queen Latifah not only starred in the 2005 movie *Beauty Shop*, a spinoff of *Barbershop 2*, she also co-produced the film. Here, she reprises her character from *Barbershop*, Gina, in a scene with actress Alicia Silverstone.

❝What there isn't much of is a plot. You may not miss it. There's something about a mean building-code inspector and Jorge's revenge, but it's drowned out by the formidable old school/new school soundtrack, the tired but foolproof wisecracks, the air of you-go-girl camaraderie, and Latifah's genial authority. The breakthroughs in *Beauty Shop* are small—a heroine who's not an anorexic twig yet who still gets the guy with six-pack abs, an interracial couple who aren't that big a deal beyond prompting the comment that 'MTV is the devil' but they're there.❞

Another vehicle for Queen Latifah was *Last Holiday*, released in 2006, in which she played a New Orleans store clerk who learns she has only a few weeks to live. LL Cool J played her boyfriend, who must cope with her as she comes to terms with her diagnosis and her desire to live her remaining days to the fullest. As in many of her movies, Queen Latifah served as a means for people around her to loosen their **inhibitions**. It's a role she told the *Dallas Morning News* that she enjoys playing on and off screen.

In the romantic comedy *Last Holiday* (2006), Queen Latifah played a woman who has been misdiagnosed with a fatal illness. Her costar was LL Cool J, another hip-hop star who successfully moved into an acting career.

"People are way too wound up, and they don't even want to be. They want someone like me to come along and help them get loose and give them an excuse to do it. I find that people have more in common than they think. We just allow all this petty stuff like race and class and religion to separate us. If you just cut through the crap to who's underneath, you can make a connection."

Last Holiday was shot in New Orleans, Louisiana, an area that was later hit hard by Hurricane Katrina and underserved by government relief agencies in its aftermath. Like many Americans, Queen Latifah was touched by the plight of the people of New Orleans, who had welcomed her to their city for the filming. She hosted a BET telethon that benefited the city and gave $100,000 to the Red Cross. In addition, she supplied housing in Atlanta to some of the people she met during her stay in New Orleans. As always, Queen Latifah looked for ways to repay the community that helped make her famous.

Queen Latifah greets a crowd of her young fans after winning the Wannabe Award at the 2005 Nickelodeon Kids' Choice Awards. The award is given to a film, television, or music star that children say they "wanna be" like.

6

Role Model for Kids

In addition to being recognized and awarded by her peers, in 2005 Queen Latifah got a personal honor from the children of the United States. She was the recipient of the 2005 Kids' Choice Wannabe Award. This marked her as the celebrity American children most wanted to be like when they grow up.

The award was presented to Queen Latifah by actress Halle Berry in front of a live audience of 10,000 young people, many of whom had voted for her because of her work as a recording artist and actress and her association with children's charities. The Wannabe award came after Queen Latifah had been named Harvard Foundation's 2003 Artist of the Year for her contributions to society and the entertainment world. While being selected as a role model is a tremendous honor, it can also be a heavy burden for anyone to carry. Back in 1997 Queen Latifah told a reporter from *Rolling Stone*:

"If you can look at someone and take something positive from what they're doing, that's cool. But to be like them means you're going to do what they do, positive or negative. And nobody's perfect. If me being a role model means I can go in front of 200 kids and motivate them to stay in school, that's cool. But if I get caught driving around in a car with a gun and some marijuana [which happened to Latifah], does that mean you're all going to go ride around in a car with a gun and marijuana? I'm grown, and I made that decision for my reasons, and I have to live with the consequences of it. In an ideal world, your parents would be your role models."

These awards are evidence of Queen Latifah's commitment to community service. For example, she helps run a scholarship foundation named for her brother that awards money for college to hundreds of needy teenagers. The Lancelot H. Owens Scholarship Foundation also provides minority high school students with **mentors**, career counseling, and assistance in finding internships, summer jobs, and jobs after graduation. She also hopes one day to start community centers to give children in her hometown of Newark a place to go after school.

Queen Latifah is also working with the Curvation Project Confidence Awards, a nationwide search for women who exude confidence. Queen Latifah is the celebrity spokesperson for Curvation, an underwear company. "I credit much of who I am today to the confidence I was given as a child," she said. "Strong, independent women like my mother and grandmother showed me the power of believing in myself. Now I want to pass this message on. By helping women build their confidence, we help them live more fulfilling lives."

Once ashamed of her body, Queen Latifah is proud that *People* magazine named her one of the "50 Most Beautiful People" in 2003, putting her in the same company as Usher, Jennifer Lopez, Julia Roberts, and Halle Berry. "I think for people who may be thicker, you know, or people who may be darker, and people who may be female, it's good to see someone like me in one of the magazines under 'beautiful' so that a girl out there can say, 'You know what? I'm beautiful. She's beautiful. That must make me beautiful,'" she told *CBS News*.

A believer in tolerance and accepting other people as they are, she has helped raise money to promote understanding of gays and lesbians through concert appearances. She has also appeared in public service announcements to encourage young people to vote. In an interview with *Jet*, she said:

> **"Sometimes you've got to challenge young people. Sometimes you need to light a fire under them to see how effective things can be when you vote. We shouldn't have to beg somebody to vote. People really died so that you can vote and went through lots of changes just for you to have this right. People need to remember that."**

More than 300 women, including Queen Latifah, salute the Statue of Liberty during the Curvation Walk of Confidence in New York City, June 2004. Queen Latifah serves as a celebrity spokesperson for the underwear company.

❝We have so much power that we are wasting, it's pathetic. People count on our apathy. They win campaigns based on our apathy, knowing that we're not going to vote. If there is going to be a change made, you must vote. Even if you don't feel that your own vote counts, that's cool, but vote anyway. Just see what happens. You'll have a lot of people being real shocked right out of their jobs because they didn't think you would do it.❞

Giving Others a Shot

Mindful of the leg up she received when she was new to the entertainment industry, Queen Latifah has made it a point to promote new talent wherever she finds it. In 1992 she and her high school geometry buddy, Shakim Compere, began Flavor Unit Entertainment, a business that manages other rap stars and produces movies. The company was recently involved in the production of several films including *Bad Girls*, a vehicle for Jada Pinkett Smith, as well as *My Wife is a Gangster* and *Kidnapped*. Queen Latifah has used the company as a platform to give African Americans a shot at entertainment jobs for which people of color often find themselves shut out. In fact, she insists on having blacks working on the sets of the movies she produces. It's one of her contributions to the fight against racism. She told *ABC News*:

❝Every time I try to flag down a cab and it goes past me and picks up that white lady instead of me, that's racism. And I hate that. Or what's worse is, I'm nobody until you see that credit card, with that name on it. Or until the person next to you says, 'Do you know who that is? It's Queen Latifah.' Oh, now I'm somebody. Now you gonna stop following me around this . . . store.❞

Through Flavor Unit Entertainment, Queen Latifah has managed the careers of several rappers and rap groups, among them Naughty by Nature, OutKast, LL Cool J, Next, Monica, and SWV. As she told a *New York Times* reporter, "Before the acting business kicks in, I'm a music lover. It frustrates me to hear powerful home-grown artists that don't

Actress Jada Pinkett Smith stands with Queen Latifah at a party, January 2003. Queen Latifah's Flavor Unit Entertainment helped produce *Bad Girls*, an upcoming film from Paramount that will star both Pinkett Smith and Queen Latifah as detectives.

Although Queen Latifah's career has been wildly successful so far, the rapper-turned-actress has no plans to slow down. In recent interviews, she has spoken about the numerous things she'd still like to accomplish in show business.

make it and these demos are banging. Not just rap, but emo, rock, club, etc. Believe me, it's a tough business."

Queen Latifah's mom and dad both work for the company, which is headquartered in Jersey City. Their presence helps to keep her from believing her own hype. When she visits her mother's house, for example, she is still asked to walk her mother's dog and take out the trash. "So I walk the dog and pick up poop. And all that highfalutin stuff means nothing," she said in a 2005 interview with *Ebony*.

Remembering Her Roots

With success in so many other areas, Queen Latifah has never forgotten her roots. She admits to being a rapper at heart. "I don't think anything will give me the satisfaction of being on a stage and rockin' a crowd," she told *Ladies Home Journal* in 2002. "When it's you and the audience and you are connecting, that's just *real*."

It has been several years since Queen Latifah recorded her last rap album. Indeed, with so much going on in her life, she admits to neglecting her hip-hop side. And yet, in a 2006 interview with the Associated Press, Queen Latifah said she still hopes to release another rap record. She said:

"I've never stopped writing, but I have so much going on inside of me. I just need to take the moment and put my energies to what's happening right now right then. I have to streamline. I would love to talk about putting out another rap record. [LL Cool J] gave me a great idea that I'm not going to tell you. But I'm always gonna be a hip-hop head for life."

1970   Dana Elaine Owens born March 18 in Newark, New Jersey.

1978   Takes the name Latifah, meaning delicate and sensitive.

1987   Cuts a demo, "Princess of the Posse."

1988   Signs a recording contract with Tommy Boy Records.

1989   Debut album, *All Hail the Queen*, released by Tommy Boy.

1991   Second album, *Nature of a Sista*, is released; receives small roles in two films, *House Party 2* and *Jungle Fever*.

1992   Brother Lancelot dies in a motorcycle accident.

1993   Album *Black Reign* is released by Motown Records; chosen for the cast of the Fox television show *Living Single*. She plays the character of Khadijah James throughout the show's four-year run.

1994   Wins a Grammy Award for her single "U.N.I.T.Y."

1995   Victim of a carjacking in Harlem, during which a friend is shot.

1996   Appears in the movie *Set It Off* with Jada Pinkett Smith, Vivica Fox, and Kimberly Elise; arrested for speeding, marijuana possession, and carrying a concealed weapon.

1998   Releases *Order in the Court* on the Motown Records label.

1999   The first episode of *The Queen Latifah Show* airs; the daytime talk show runs until 2001.

2002   Arrested for reckless driving and put on three years' probation; draws critical praise for her role as Mama Morton in the hit musical *Chicago*.

2003   Nominated for Academy Award for Best Supporting Actress in *Chicago*.

2004   *The Dana Owens Album*, featuring jazz, soul, and pop standards, is released.

2005   Appears in the movies *Barbershop 2* and *The Cookout*.

2006   Received a star on the Hollywood Walk of Fame; praised for her role in the film *Last Holiday*.

Albums

1989	*All Hail the Queen*
1991	*Nature of a Sista*
1993	*Black Reign*
1998	*Order in the Court*
2002	*She's a Queen: A Collection of Hits*
2004	*The Dana Owens Album*

Selected Films

1991   *House Party 2*
       Jungle Fever

1992   *Juice*

1993   *My Life*

1996   *Set It Off*

1997   *Hoodlum*

1998   *Sphere*
       Living Out Loud

1999   *The Bone Collector*
       Bringing Out the Dead (voice)

2002   *The Country Bears*
       Brown Sugar
       Chicago

2003   *Bringing Down the House*
       Scary Movie 3

2004   *Taxi*
       Barbershop 2
       The Cookout

2005   *Beauty Shop*

2006   *Last Holiday*
       Ice Age 2 (voice)
       Hairspray

Awards and Recognition

1992   Nominated, Grammy Award for Best Rap Solo Performance, *All Hail the Queen.*

1994   Winner, Grammy Award for Best Rap Solo Performance for "U.N.I.T.Y."

Winner, NAACP Image Award and Soul Train Music Award for "U.N.I.T.Y."

1995   Winner, Soul Train Sammy Davis Jr. Entertainer of the Year Award.

1997   Winner, Aretha Franklin Entertainer of the Year Award, *Soul Train* Lady of Soul Awards.

2003   Named one of the 50 Most Beautiful People by *People.*

Nominated, Golden Globe Award and Academy Award for Best Supporting Actress, *Chicago.*

Winner, SAG Award as member of Best Ensemble Cast Performance, *Chicago.*

2005   Winner, Wannabe Award at Kids' Choice Awards Show.

2006   Awarded star on Hollywood Walk of Fame.

Collier, Aldore. "A Royal Rap: Queen Latifah Reigns on and off TV."
Ebony 49, no. 2, p. 118.

Graham, Renee. "Queen Latifah Is in Danger of Losing Her Crown."
Boston Globe, April 8, 2003.

Pough, Gwendolyn D. *Check It While I Wreck It: Black Womanhood,
Hip-Hop Culture, and the Public Sphere.* Boston: Northeastern
University Press, 2004.

"Queen Latifah Says 'There's Life after *Living Single.*'" *Jet Magazine* 94,
no. 8, p. 34.

Queen Latifah, with Karen Hunter. *Ladies First: Revelations of a Strong
Woman.* New York: William Morrow and Company, 1999.

Rader, Dotson. "Take The Punch—But Then Get Up Again." *Parade*,
March 6, 2005.

Sinclair, Tom. "Best Supporting Actress: Queen Latifah: *Chicago.*"
Entertainment Weekly, February 21, 2003, p. 52.

Smith, Dinitia. "The Queen of Rap: Latifah Sells 'Womanism.'"
New York 23, no. 47, p. 124.

Tracy, Kathleen. *Queen Latifah.* Hockessin, Delaware: Mitchell Lane
Publishers, 2005.

Web Sites
www.eurweb.com
Urban radio legend Lee Bailey's Web site provides daily updates on
Queen Latifah and other black entertainment figures.

www.lastholidaymovie.com
Official Web site for the movie *Last Holiday.* Watch a movie trailer,
read a synopsis of the film, and find out information about the cast.

www.lhosf.org
Web site of the Lancelot H. Owens Scholarship Foundation, which
includes more information about the life of Queen Latifah's brother
as well as qualifications for receiving financial aid through the
organization.

www.miramax.com/chicago

Web site for the movie *Chicago*, which includes a 30-minute documentary on the making of the movie.

www.queenlatifah.com

Queen Latifah's official Web site offers cuts from *The Dana Owens Album* and the opportunity to sign up for a newsletter to receive updates on the star.

www.seeing-stars.com/Immortalized/WalkOfFame.shtml

Learn more about the Hollywood Walk of Fame including trivia, history, and where to find individual stars.

anthem—song that serves as a theme for a nation or social movement.

feminist—person concerned about women's rights, often identifying with the feminist movement born in the 1960s.

impresario—a person who stages entertainment, such as a concert promoter.

inhibitions—fears that cause people to hold back and not be themselves.

jam sessions—term for an informal gathering of musicians who improvise on their instruments.

lesbian—woman who is sexually attracted to other women.

lyrics—the words to a song.

mainstream—the actions, values, and ideas that are most widely accepted by members of a group or society.

mentor—a person, usually older and more experienced, who provides advice and support to young people to help them succeed.

ovation—sustained applause.

persona—an identity or role that somebody presents to the rest of the world.

probation—status granted to a criminal defendant that permits him to serve a sentence outside of jail.

producer—person responsible for raising funds to make a movie and for hiring people to work on the film.

stereotype—an oversimplified, often negative, image or idea about a particular group or class of people.

Gail Snyder is a freelance writer and advertising copywriter who has written six books for young readers. She lives in Chalfont, Pennsylvania, with her husband, Hal, and daughters Michelle and Ashley.

Picture Credits

page

2: KRT/Giulio Marcocchi
8: UPI Photo/Jim Ruymen
11: Kathy Hutchins/Hutchins Photo
12: Kathy Hutchins/Hutchins Photo
14: Zumma Press/Rena Durham
17: Zumma Press/Rena Durham
18: NMI/Michelle Feng
21: Warner Brothers/
Everrett Collection
22: KRT/Richard Corkery
24: NMI/Michelle Feng
27: NMI
29: KRT/NMI
30: Zuma Press/Laura Farr/NMI

32: KRT/NMI
35: NMI/Michelle Feng
36: Warner Brothers/
Everrett Collection
38: KRT/Lionel Hahn
41: KRT/Tracy Bennett
42: KRT/Mindy Schauer
44: Disney Pictures/NMI
45: MGM/NMI
46: Paramount Pictures/KRT
48: Reuters/Fred Prouser
51: PRNewsFoto/NMI
53: Zuma Press/Rena Durham
54: PRNewsFoto/NMI

Front cover: Tim Goodwin/Star Max
Back cover: Zuma Press/Tina Fultz